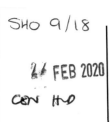

D0306329

Max's mission log

We are travelling through space on board the micro-ship Excelsa with our new friends, Nok and Seven.

We're on a mission to save Planet Exis (Nok's home planet), which is running out of power. The only way to do this is to collect the fragments that form the Core of Exis – the most powerful energy source in the galaxy.

So far we have collected four fragments, but we need to find a fifth! Only the king and queen of Exis (Nok's parents) know where the final fragment is hidden, so our next task is to find them. It's not easy. A space villain called Badlaw wants the power of the Core for himself.

Fragments collected so far: 4

In our last adventure ...

We followed a clue left by the king and queen. It led us to Planet Ariddas, a planet of giant creatures called Ariddians. They thought we would make good pets!

The Ariddians put us in a cage and, just when we thought it couldn't get any worse, the Krools arrived! Luckily, the Ariddians thought the Krools were balls and started playing with them.

As we were making our escape, we found another clue from the king and queen. We are now on our way to Planet Spongemar where our search for them will continue.

Chapter 1 – The warning

On course for Planet Spongemar, the Excelsa zoomed through space at super-charged speed.

Max glanced round at the others. Cat, Ant and Tiger looked tired. Seven was OK – robots didn't need much rest. Nok just looked sad.

"I'm sure we'll find your parents soon, Nok," said Max, trying to reassure his friend. "Then we can get the fifth fragment and sort things out back on Exis."

"It will take hours to reach Planet Spongemar," said Cat, yawning. "There's a lot of empty space to cross first."

Suddenly the sound of snarls and snorts blasted from the ship's speakers.

Tiger shuddered. "Scary alien voice alert!"

Ant leaned closer to his screen. "It's coming from nearby. I'm scanning the area ahead. Magnifying image ..."

A strange, spiky object appeared on the viewscreen. It was floating in space.

Seven recognized the object immediately. "It's a deep-space warning beacon."

"A warning beacon?" asked Cat worriedly.

"The beacon is transmitting a message in lots of different languages. I will try to translate it for us." Seven whirred and hummed. Then he said in a strange-sounding voice, "Beware! Danger ahead ... sirens ... listen or else ..."

"Sirens?" Tiger frowned. "Like ambulance sirens? I can't hear any."

"Does it say what the danger is, Seven?" asked Max.

"No. The message is incomplete," said Seven in his normal voice. "It's a very old machine."

"Well, we can't turn back now," said Max firmly. "Stay alert, everyone!"

Chapter 2 – The Sirens

The ship zoomed past the warning beacon into the black depths of space. The friends waited tensely as the minutes crept by.

Suddenly, a craggy lump of rock appeared on the viewscreen.

"It looks like an asteroid," said Nok.

Cat peered at her monitor. "I think there's something on top of it. Can we take a closer look?"

As the Excelsa drew nearer, Max and the others could see three weird, green creatures perched on the space rock. They looked part-dragon and part-bird with their long, colourful wings.

The dragon-birds opened their mouths. At once, the ship was filled with eerie singing. As if under a spell, the micro-friends stopped what they were doing.

Tiger looked dreamy. "It sounds ... lovely."

"Beautiful," Ant agreed.

The song's melody was hypnotic even though the words were alien.

Cat yawned noisily, and Nok rubbed his eyes.

"It's like a lullaby," he said, with a sigh.

"I'm sleepy," yawned Max.

"No! You must all keep alert!" cried Seven. "Don't you know the old Earth legend about strange, singing creatures that lived in the sea? They were called Sirens. The Sirens' hypnotic songs made sailors fall asleep, so they crashed into rocks and were shipwrecked! They must be what the beacon was warning us about."

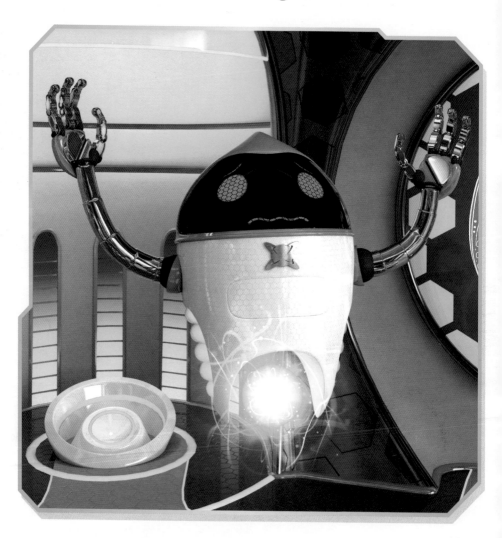

"You think these *space* Sirens are trying to make us crash?" said Max, sitting up.

"Not if I can help it!" said Nok, shaking the song from his head and pulling on the steering orbs.

The ship zoomed up, away from the Sirens. Their singing became a faint echo in the distance.

"Phew! It's stopping ..." said Cat.

Her relief didn't last long.

Chapter 3 – Flight into danger

Ahead of them, many more huge, lumpy rocks were coming into sight.

"We're flying into an asteroid field!" Tiger yelled.

"We must slow down," said Nok. "If we crashed into one of those giant rocks we'd be finished!"

Ant pulled back on the acceleration lever. Immediately, the whine of the engines settled to a gentle hum.

As they slowed, the spooky singing drifted
through the ship once more. Within moments,
the micro-friends felt sleepy again.

Cat's eyelids fluttered as she struggled to focus
on her screen. She shook her head and blinked,
trying to clear her vision. There were three
flashing dots getting closer to the Excelsa.

"The Sirens are chasing us!" she said.

"What can we do, Seven?" asked Ant.

"I will try and translate their language," said Seven. "Maybe we can ask them to stop singing. If they knew how important our mission was they might let us pass safely."

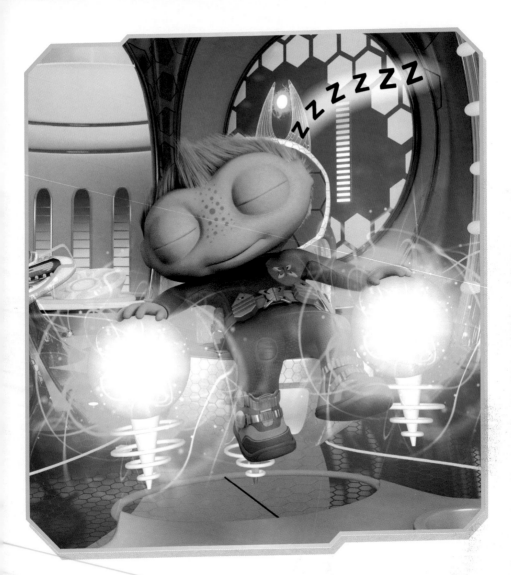

"Hurry, Seven," said Max, wearily. "I can't stay awake much longer, and look at Nok!" Max lifted a heavy arm and pointed at his friend.

Nok was snoring softly, slumped in his seat, but his hands were still on the steering orbs. He was steering in his sleep!

Suddenly, *CRASH! BOOM!* Two asteroids smashed together with crushing force just in front of the ship. The deafening noise jolted Nok awake.

"What happened?" he said, blinking.

"I don't know," said Max. "The asteroids seem to be moving by themselves!"

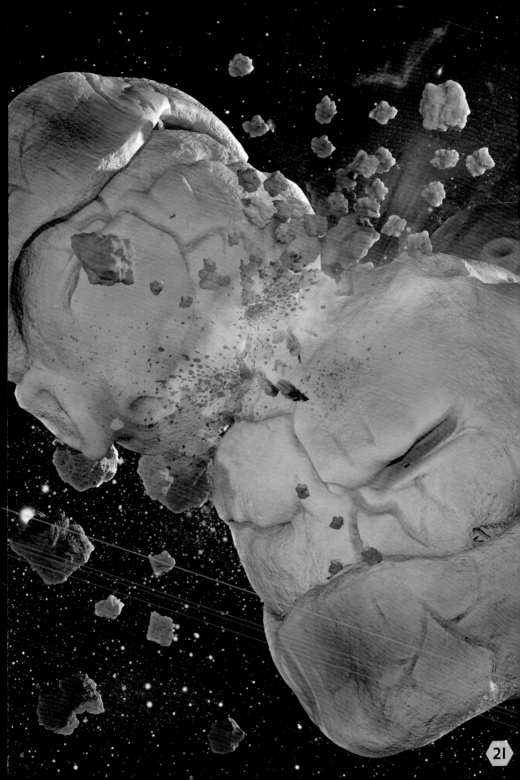

21

Almost immediately, the Sirens came back into view. They flew alongside the ship. As they flapped their scaly wings, their singing grew even louder.

Max covered his ears. "Try not to listen, everyone!"

With horror, Tiger saw more and more asteroids tumbling around ahead of them. Then two of them stopped in front of the ship.

"I don't think they are ordinary asteroids," he said, pointing grimly at the viewscreen. "Look!"

Burning yellow caverns opened up in the rocks. They were eyes ... and they were glaring angrily at the Excelsa!

Chapter 4 – The living rocks

Ant slammed on the space-brakes.

The bottom of the rocks cracked open to reveal mouths crammed full of stalactite and stalagmite teeth.

"Those rocks are *ALIVE!*" cried Cat.

"Living rocks?" Seven searched his computer brain. "They must be ... Craggrox! Beings made of solid stone. It's not an asteroid field. It's a colony of Craggrox!"

Craggrox

Craggrox are boulders with brains. They spend most of their time asleep. A colony of sleeping Craggrox can look just like a normal asteroid field, but beware as they are very grumpy if woken unexpectedly. Keep away from Craggrox at all cost!

Diet

Craggrox live on space dust, planet rings and stray spaceships.

Habitat

They live in colonies all across the Beta-Prime Galaxy.

burning eyes ●○○○○○○○○

large ears ●○●○●○●○●

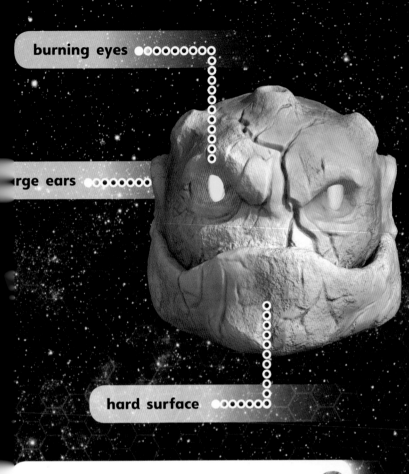

hard surface ●○●○●○●

Do not disturb!

Craggrox have big, cave-like ears which are very sensitive to noise. They like peace and quiet. The noise of passing spaceships is painful and they react by attacking them!

The Sirens swooped in on one side of the micro-ship while the fierce-looking Craggrox gathered on the other.

"We're in so much trouble," said Cat, "but all I want to do is sleep."

The Sirens' singing was louder than ever.

Max felt his eyelids drooping again. "Have you finished translating the Sirens' language yet, Seven? Can you understand what they are saying?"

"I'm afraid not," Seven replied. "It's a very ancient language."

"Then you must keep us awake. You are the only one not affected."

"Um ..." Seven tried to concentrate over the noise of the Sirens. "How about a joke? I say, I say, I say, what kind of saddle do you put on a space-pony? A saddle-lite! Get it? Like a satellite, only — "

Nok rolled his eyes. "That's terrible!" he said. "Tell us another."

Seven thought hard. "How does a solar system hold up its trousers? With an asteroid belt!"

"Don't mention asteroids!" Max groaned.

"Then how about some music?" asked Seven. A loud, pounding tune started to thump from Seven's head. His eyes flashed like disco lights. He flipped upside down and started to spin.

BOOM! The Excelsa lurched to the side as a Craggrox bumped against it. Seven fell over and his music stopped.

Max glanced around the bridge. "Everyone OK?" They all nodded sleepily. "Ant, run a damage report," Max continued.

Forcing his eyes wide open, Ant slowly tapped the controls on his desk and waited. "We were lucky. The ship's OK."

Max lifted his head and looked at the front viewscreen. "I don't know about lucky ... look!"

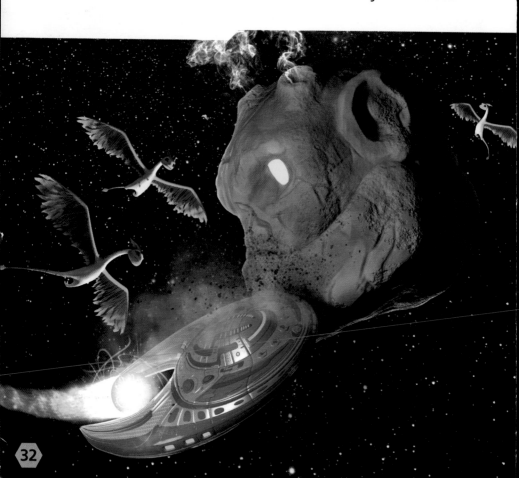

Chapter 5 – The song's secret

The Sirens flew right in front of the ship and stopped singing. They stared in with pleading eyes.

"I think they're trying to tell us something," said Ant.

Seven's computer brain whirred. "I should be able to tell you. The language translation is now complete." He paused for a moment, lost in thought. "You are right, Ant. I was wrong. They are trying to help us, not make us crash. Listen to their song."

Seven cleared his electronic throat:

"Sleep, oh little ones! Will you not sleep?
We are the guardians of the deep.
Will you not heed our warning tune?
We will guard you from Craggrox doom.
The noise of your spaceship hurts
their brains.
They'll crush you 'til only junk remains.
So, sleep, oh, little ones, open your ears.
Let soothing sleep replace your fears.
Only then can we steer you through,
Just as Nok's parents trusted us to!"

"Wow! The Sirens have seen my parents," said Nok.

"They aren't bad after all." Cat smiled. They must have helped the king and queen get past the Craggrox."

"The Sirens know the safe path," Seven agreed. "Unfortunately they can only guide spaceship pilots who are asleep."

"We have to trust the Sirens," said Max. "Time for a nap, Nok," he joked, but his friend was already dropping off.

Sirens

Information

Space sirens are the guardians of space, but they are rare so you are lucky if you encounter one. They warn travellers of danger. They have beautiful voices. They send pilots of spaceships to sleep by singing so that they can guide the ships to safety.

Diet
Sirens live on space plankton.

Habitat
Sirens can be found on the outskirts of areas of danger (such as Craggrox colonies).

large eyes ●●○○○○○○○○○○○○○○○○○

colourful wings ●○○○○○○○○○○○

Space guardians

Sirens are helpful creatures. They use warning beacons to send messages to approaching ships. Each message is translated into over 10,000 alien languages.

Max turned to Seven. "Can you relay a message to the Sirens?"

"I can try," said Seven, pushing a button on the control panel.

"Tell them we're sorry," Max said. "We understand what they were trying to do now. Ask them if they will still help us."

Out of the viewscreen the micro-friends saw the Sirens smile and nod. They sang again, more sweetly than ever. Max, Cat, Ant and Tiger began to yawn.

"I will wake you at once if anything goes wrong," Seven promised.

This time, the children gave in to the Sirens' song. They let the music soothe them and within seconds they were fast asleep. Guided by the Sirens, Nok's hands moved confidently at the controls.

The Sirens helped Nok steer the Excelsa through the living asteroid maze. The Craggrox gnashed their terrible teeth as the spaceship sped past. It was an amazing, scary sight but only Seven was awake to witness it.

Finally, the ship soared past the last of the Craggrox. The Craggrox roared angrily. Their rocky brains were sore from the noise of the spaceship.

Once out of danger, Seven spoke to the Sirens in their language. "Your warning beacon is worn out," he explained. "We couldn't hear the complete message."

"Thank you for telling us," sang the Sirens. "That explains why the king and queen resisted us at first, too."

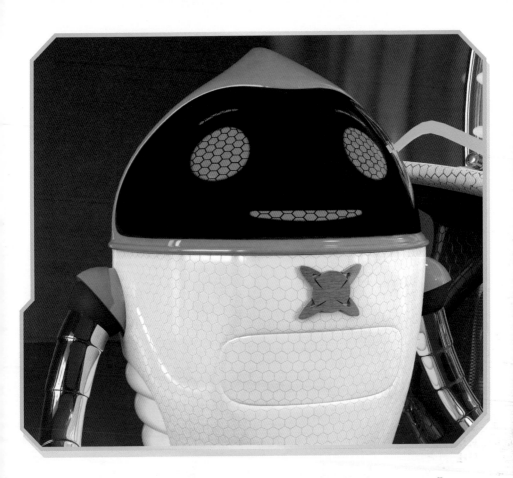

"We are trying to find the king and queen," Seven said. "Do you know where they were going when they left you?"

"We believe they were on their way to Spongemar," the Sirens replied.

"That is good news. It confirms what we thought too. When were they here?" asked Seven.

"Only two days ago," the Sirens replied. "Good luck on your mission to find them."

"Thank you," Seven sang back in reply.

The Sirens stopped singing. Slowly, the micro-friends began to wake up.

"Did we make it?" Ant said, yawning.

"We certainly did," said Seven. "Thanks to the Sirens."

"We're safe again!" Tiger laughed. "We've had a good sleep, too!"

Seven turned to Nok. "Best of all, the sirens have seen your parents. They were here only two days ago."

Nok grinned. "We're catching up with them!"

"It's a good job," said Max. "We must get hold of that fifth fragment – before it's too late."

As the Excelsa sped on its way towards Spongemar, the Sirens waved goodbye. Then they flew swiftly back to their home among the sleeping Craggrox.

Find out what happens next in *Attack of the Blobs*.